Lolly's Picnic

By Laura Crisafulli Kennedy
Illustrated by Jamie Forgetta

Lolly's Picnic

By

Laura Crisafulli Kennedy

Illustrated by Jamie Forgetta

Lolly's Picnic.

Copyright © 2015 Laura Crisafulli Kennedy. Produced and printed by Stillwater River Publications. All rights reserved. Written and produced in the United States of America. This book may not be reproduced or sold in any form without the expressed, written permission of the author and publisher.

Visit our website **at www.StillwaterPress.com** for more information.

First Stillwater River Publications Edition

ISBN-10: 0-692-47956-2
ISBN-13: 978-069247956-8

Library of Congress Control Number: 2015945266

1 2 3 4 5 6 7 8 9 10
Written by Laura Crisafulli Kennedy
Original Illustrations by Jamie Forgetta
Cover design by Dawn M. Porter
Published by Stillwater River Publications, Glocester, RI, USA

To Tyler, Hannah and Tristan...

and to all the young at heart...

May you always believe in your own Magic!!

Lolly woke up to a beautiful sun-shining morning. She jumped out of bed, smiled and danced around her room. "What a perfect day for a picnic" she said happily!

Lolly gathered up her favorite toys, packed up her blanket and was happily on her way to her favorite picnic spot.

As Lolly laid out her blanket and began to unpack her toys, she remembered that tomorrow she would be moving to her new home. Lolly suddenly felt very sad and scared.

"Maybe this picnic isn't such a good idea" Lolly said aloud. "I just don't feel like having fun." She started to cry.

Lolly's toys looked on. They didn't like to see her so upset. It just wasn't right.

Oliver the Octopus was the first to speak. "Don't cry Lolly. We have had so many smiles and great times on all of our other adventures. This one will be grand too. We always find a way."

Oliver danced around Lolly, swinging his tentacles and singing:

"Here we go, here we go, on to our next adventure.
What will we see, what will we do, who will we meet?
Oh goodness, all this excitement, all these new things.
But isn't that the fun of it? It makes it such a treat!"

Lolly giggled and clapped at his song. Oliver's rhymes were so silly, he could always make Lolly laugh.

Lolly smiled as she remembered the time Oliver was dancing and twirling around so much that his tentacles got all jumbled up. Oliver never minded. He just picked himself up and kept on singing.

"I know Oliver," Lolly said, "we have had such fun on our adventures so far, but I am just not sure about this one." Lolly paused and continued sadly, "what if I can't have fun, what if I forget how to smile?"

Oliver swished around Lolly making her giggle again for a moment. "Then just imagine your smile and the happy things in your heart. That is how to start," he sang.

Lolly knew Oliver was right. Oliver loved trying new things. Lolly could always count on Oliver for an exciting adventure. She shook her head and sighed.

"What if nobody likes me or wants to be my friend?"

"What will I do?" Lolly questioned.

Kirby the Cat strolled onto the blanket holding his head up and wiggling his tail in the air. Kirby loved to prance around this way. Lolly was happy to see him.

"Lolly, my friend, always hold your head up high - it is easier to see this way. Come on Lolly, do what I do and follow me!"

Kirby and Lolly were prancing around the blanket holding their heads up high.

"Don't you feel better already Lolly?" Kirby purred. "You will make friends because you are wonderful through and through. Believe that always and it will always be true."

Kirby and Lolly continued prancing around.

"Now you can teach your new friends." Kirby said.

Lolly still looked sad.

"Look at me Lolly." Kirby said firmly. "You are strong, kind, smart and filled with courage. This is what I see when I look at you and others will too. You are special Lolly, inside and out."

Lolly stroked Kirby and smiled. She could always count on Kirby to make her feel better. She closed her eyes tight and wished for enough luck to make everything alright. "Please, please, please," she whispered, "let everything work out!"

Lolly opened her eyes just in time to see Lucky the Ladybug landing on her hand. "Lucky here! Ladybug Lucky is my name - you called?"
Lucky saw Lolly's sad face and listened to her story. "Perhaps I can help too," she said and smiled. "Here is one of my spots."

Lucky removed a spot from her back and gave it to Lolly. "Use this wisely, Lolly, luck only gets you so far. It's the hard times that can make you strong and you are luckier when you are strong!" Lucky exclaimed and continued. "Believe me, I earned my spots by being strong and brave. Now I can share them with you."

Lolly held the spot. "How do you become strong and brave?" she asked her new friend.

"HMMM," Lucky thought about this for a moment. "Sometimes being strong and brave means finding a way not to be afraid. Sometimes it means believing in something even when it is hard to believe and sometimes it means standing up for what you think is right. There are so many ways to be strong."

Lucky was so excited to share her thoughts with Lolly. She really wanted to help her. Lucky continued, "I can see that you are strong Lolly but you need to believe."

Lolly listened to her new friend. "You may not have spots on the outside like I do," Lucky whispered in her ear, "but you have them inside - those count too!" Lucky smiled and flew away.

That was very lucky indeed thought Lolly.

Lolly was beginning to believe all of the things she was
hearing. She was beginning to feel hopeful, which made her smile.

At that very moment, Magic the Witch arrived, waving her wand and filling the picnic blanket with sparkles and glitter.

"These are your dreams and wishes Lolly. Gather them up and believe in their magic." Magic the Witch smiled. "You have so much magic Lolly! It is always there to sparkle and glitter!"

Magic waved her wand. "Look, look, look and you will see!" Sparkles and glitter were flying everywhere. Magic continued "... and when you aren't sure, just say 'I believe in me!' "

Lolly's eyes opened wide with fascination! What a beautiful sight. What a magical day this was turning out to be!

Just when Lolly thought things couldn't get any better, BellaBear, Lolly's favorite teddy, climbed onto her lap.

"Lolly," BellaBear said as she nestled close to Lolly, "I've learned my best hugs from you - hugs filled with love, love, love. You always take such good care of me. Hug me now Lolly and hold on tight."

Lolly hugged her bear tightly and her heart filled with love and happiness. Lolly forgot all about being sad.

Lolly's picnic continued all day until the sun began to set.

Lolly and her toys giggled and played and danced and sang.

Lolly was happy and feeling brave and strong thanks to a little help from her friends. She was ready for her new day and all the adventures it could bring.

At the end of the day, Lolly lay down with all of her toy friends gathered near. She gave them all one last squeeze before she closed her eyes. "I am going to be fine," she mumbled. "Even better than fine!" Lolly smiled and fell fast asleep.

ABOUT THE AUTHOR

Laura Crisafulli Kennedy was born in Bronx, New York, and moved to Rhode Island with her family when she was six. She currently resides in Smithfield, RI, with her husband, John, and her children, Hannah and Tristan.

Laura thoroughly enjoys writing and being a mom. It has been a dream of hers, since childhood, to write a children's book. The idea for her story and characters developed over time culminating into this story when her children were young.

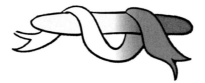

ABOUT THE ILLUSTRATOR

"As long as I am doing some form of art I am happy" is how Jamie Forgetta feels in regard to life. A Rhode Island born artist, she discovered her love of drawing at a young age when she would draw her favorite cartoon characters and trace pictures from different kid's books. She graduated from Pratt Institute where she majored in 3D animation, despite this she found a stronger love for the two dimensional form of storytelling. She lives to bring the same joy to others that art brought to her.

Made in the USA
Middletown, DE
19 November 2015